To

_____

From

_____

Date

_____

I Love You, God

Written and Illustrated by P.K. Hallinan

HARVEST HOUSE PUBLISHERS

EUGENE, OREGON

I LOVE YOU, GOD
Text Copyright © 2010 by P.K. Hallinan
Artwork Copyright © 2010 by P.K. Hallinan
Published by Harvest House Publishers
Eugene, Oregon 97402
www.harvesthousepublishers.com

ISBN 978-0-7369-2717-8

Original artwork by P.K. Hallinan

Design and production by Harvest House Publishers, Eugene, Oregon

Printed in China

10 11 12 13 14 15 16 / LP-NI / 10 9 8 7 6 5 4 3 2 1

For children everywhere
who want God to know
how much they love Him.

—P.K.

I love You, God,

and I'm happy to do

whatever brings honor

and glory to You!

I try to be nice to the people I know.

I try to be patient when things go too slow.

I like to be helpful so others might see

a glimpse of the light You've ignited in me!

I love You, God, in so many ways—

I can't wait for Sundays to sing out Your praise!

I offer my friendship to each girl and boy.

I give what I can to bring comfort and joy.

I listen to others who need to be heard.

I strive to be honest in deed and in word.

I visit my friends who are ailing or blue,

then prayerfully ask for a healing or two.

And I always say grace when supper is served.

My thanks for Your feast is the least You deserve.

I love You, God,

for all that You give.

Each season's a reason

to laugh and to live!

I try not to judge what I hear or I see.

I don't hold a grudge—or let it hold me!

I reach out my hand during life's little trials.

I do what I can to turn frowns into smiles.

And I honor my parents and my grandparents too,

for helping me see how to be more like You!

I love You, God, for all that You've done.

My cup's overflowing, and You've only begun!

So, I'll look to Your Bible for the answers I need.

I'll find little diamonds in the verses I read.

I'll share how You died

and then rose from the grave

to free us from sin

so our souls could be saved.

And I'll mention with glee

how Your love comforts me.

Yes, I'll worship You, God, in prayer and in song.

I'll sing of Your grace till my songs are all gone.

I'll serve You with gladness in all kinds of weather.

I love You, God...

from now till forever.

We love Him because He first loved us.

1 John 4:19